THE TALE OF
Custard the
Dragon

Ogden Nash

THE TALE OF
Custard the
Dragon

Illustrated by

Lynn Munsinger

Little, Brown and Company ✳ Boston New York Toronto London

For John, with love   L.M.

Text copyright 1936 by Ogden Nash
Renewed by Frances Nash, Isabel Nash Eberstadt, Linell Nash Smith
Illustrations copyright © 1995 by Lynn Munsinger

First Edition

Library of Congress Cataloging-in-Publication Data

Nash, Ogden, 1902–1971
The tale of Custard the Dragon / Ogden Nash ; illustrated by Lynn
Munsinger.— 1st ed.
     p. cm.
   Summary: In this humorous poem, Custard the cowardly dragon saves
the day when a pirate threatens Belinda and her pet animals.
     ISBN 0-316-59880-1
     1. Dragon — Juvenile poetry. 2. Children's poetry, American.
[1. Dragons — Poetry. 2. Humorous poetry. 3. American poetry.]
I. Munsinger, Lynn, ill. II. Title.
PS3527.A637C87   1995
811' .52 — dc20.   94-6594

10 9 8 7 6 5 4 3 2 1

NIL

Published simultaneously in Canada by Little, Brown & Company (Canada) Limited

Printed in Italy

Belinda lived in a little white house,
With a little black kitten and a little gray mouse,
And a little yellow dog and a little red wagon,
And a realio, trulio little pet dragon.

Now the name of the little black kitten was Ink,
And the little gray mouse, she called her Blink,

And the little yellow dog was sharp as Mustard,

But the dragon was a coward, and she called him Custard.

Custard the dragon had big sharp teeth,
And spikes on top of him and scales underneath,

Mouth like a fireplace, chimney for a nose,
And realio, trulio daggers on his toes.

Belinda was as brave as a barrelful of bears,
And Ink and Blink chased lions down the stairs,

Mustard was as brave as a tiger in a rage,
But Custard cried for a nice safe cage.

Belinda tickled him, she tickled him unmerciful,
Ink, Blink, and Mustard, they rudely called him Percival,
They all sat laughing in the little red wagon
At the realio, trulio cowardly dragon.

Belinda giggled till she shook the house,
And Blink said, "*Weeck!*" which is giggling for a mouse,
Ink and Mustard rudely asked his age,
When Custard cried for a nice safe cage.

Suddenly, suddenly they heard a nasty sound,
And Mustard growled, and they all looked around.
"*Meowch!*" cried Ink, and "*Ooh!*" cried Belinda,
For there was a pirate, climbing in the winda.

Pistol in his left hand, pistol in his right,
And he held in his teeth a cutlass bright,
His beard was black, one leg was wood;
It was clear that the pirate meant no good.

Belinda paled, and she cried, "Help! Help!"
But Mustard fled with a terrified yelp,

Ink trickled down to the bottom of the household,
And little mouse Blink strategically mouseholed.

But up jumped Custard, snorting like an engine,
Clashed his tail like irons in a dungeon,
With a clatter and a clank and a jangling squirm,
He went at the pirate like a robin at a worm.

The pirate gaped at Belinda's dragon,
And gulped some grog from his pocket flagon,
He fired two bullets, but they didn't hit,
And Custard gobbled him, every bit.

Belinda embraced him, Mustard licked him,
No one mourned for his pirate victim.
Ink and Blink in glee did gyrate
Around the dragon that ate the pirate.

But presently up spoke little dog Mustard:
"I'd have been twice as brave if I hadn't been flustered."
And up spoke Ink and up spoke Blink:
"We'd have been three times as brave, we think,"

And Custard said, "I quite agree
That everybody is braver than me."

Belinda still lives in her little white house,
With her little black kitten and her little gray mouse,
And her little yellow dog and her little red wagon,
And her realio, trulio little pet dragon.

Belinda is as brave as a barrelful of bears,
And Ink and Blink chase lions down the stairs,

Mustard is as brave as a tiger in a rage . . .

But Custard keeps crying for a nice safe cage.